Just a Flight Away

Farah Naaz

ISBN 979-8-89233-758-8

Contents

Acknowledgement

First and foremost, I would love to thank my parents who always supported me and always let me follow my dreams secondly my friends who always motivated me, hyped me up and always gave me a positive response throughout my writing career and third to God for providing me the skills and resources and such supportive family and friends.

Last but not the least, I would love to express gratitude towards Notion Press who gave me this opportunity to publish and circulate my thoughts all over the world.

Biography

She is **Farah Naaz, a 16-year-old** teenager **(19-03-2007)** who belongs to **Odisha** but currently residing in **Bahrain.** She started writing as her hobby but soon it turned to her passion. She loves writing poetries, quotes, novels, etc. She believes that writing down your thoughts is a great thing to do when no one is there to understand what you actually feel. It works like a therapy. She started writing at the age of 14. At a very young age she understood the depth of life and started penning down her thoughts which led her to a journey of being an author. To know more about her, you can check out her Instagram page @_.fairytalessss._

"Distance is just like a practical solution of our theoretical imagination of love to see how hard can we try to make it happen."

Love is pure, it does Not require to be physically present, even your virtual presence will make the person so Glad and thankful. True love does not calculate the distance, it just calculates the real Intention between two people. Ones the Intentions are set, there's no requirement to set any distance or boundaries.

A 20-year-old girl passionate about her work as a content creator who belongs to **Uttar Pradesh** but lives in **Bahrain**, an extrovert who love to make friends but still didn't find such a friend on whom she can rely on, share all her problems and just be the same she is.

Chapter – 1

The First Text

One beautiful Saturday evening, Mahirah was just laying down and a thought popped up in her mind that once her friend asked her about Long Distance Relationship [LDR] which most of the people have negative assumptions about that it never works, etc. Without paying much attention to it she took her phone and started checking her message requests. While scrolling down, she saw a guy's text named **Saad** [He's a young **23**-year-old guy from **Pune,** an Introverted person who just vibe with only his group of friends and usually enjoys his own company]. Little did Mahirah knew that he's her future, she would have accepted the request at the same time. But she decided to keep it as it is and clicked on his profile to view it. After viewing, she said to herself "Well, he's not my type" and clicked back to delete the request. But destiny has its own plans and she mistakenly clicked on **'Accept the request'** instead of declining it. "Oopsiee!!" She thought for a while and then replied him back.

Few hours later when Saad saw her text, he couldn't believe his eyes that his crush actually replied him and was rechecking the account again and again. He then introduced himself and both started talking.

Saad: It still feels like a dream that you've accepted my request.

Mahirah: Awww!! Thank you! That's really sweet of you

Saad: You really think so? I'm totally blushing...

Mahirah: Don't hide that blush. It lets me know my charms are working

Saad: Your charm works so well that everyone around you wants you in their team.

Mahirah: (*blushes*) ummm.... Are you flirting??

Saad: Nahh, I am not flirting. I'm just trying to be extra nice for the person who is extra charming.

Mahirah: Well that was a good one.... (*smiles*)

Although Saad never vibed up with someone so easily and early but this time things were quite different. They both talked for a while and winded up for the day. After having Conversation with Mahirah, he started admiring her even more.

He didn't want to end the conversation but at the same time he did not wanted her to feel bored too. He couldn't stop thinking about her the whole day, he had never felt the same for anyone else in his life before. It was such a strange feeling for him. Saad was not sure about anything in his life, but the only thing he was sure about that he wanted Mahirah in it. They eventually started talking everyday. Well, he didn't confess to her yet but she runs on his mind the whole day. They both now became good friends and even roast each other. It seems like roasting each other is their love language.

Mahirah: Have you heard of this song?

Saad: Which one?

Mahirah: I am a mother.

Saad: Yes, I know.

Mahirah: What the hell! I was talking about the song

Saad: But I was talking about you.

Mahirah: Wth! Do I really look that old?

Saad: Yes.

Mahirah: Seriously???

Saad: Nope, you're beautiful and you look young

Mahirah: I know, Thanks! But why am I talking to you then? Get lost!

From roasting each other to hyping up is all what they do everyday. Saad was truly enamoured with her but he knew that she doesn't feel the same and if he confesses it to her then he might lose the friendship too. So he stopped talking to her for a while and was not replying to her texts like he did before. When Mahirah noticed his strange behaviour, she got worried about it as he never behaved in such a manner before. Whenever she texts him, he doesn't give her fascinating replies which he used to do earlier. She was bothered and tensed at the same time that did he started talking to someone else? Or is he not interested to talk to her anymore? She was not sure about the feelings she's getting is just out of concern or more than that. She decided not to think much about it but whenever a notification pops us in her phone, she checks it immediately but gets disappointed seeing that it's not his text.

On the other hand, it was difficult for Saad too to refrain himself from texting her. Both of them were restless and just thinking about each other.

The next day, it was Mahirah's birthday and the only text she's been waiting for was his. And he too couldn't resist wishing her on her special day. So he wished her at sharp 12:00 am. She immediately replied him and asked about him being weird. He replied saying that it's her day today and it's not the right time now to discuss these things cuz he doesn't want to spoil her day. He was just busy with some stuffs. Mahirah was still stressed but much relieved after receiving a text from him. But Mahirah wanted to know exactly where he was busy at and if it is more important to him than her. So she asked:

Mahirah: As you said that you were busy with **"Some stuffs"**, so was this **"Some stuffs"** more important than me?

Saad: How can I explain how important you're to me? I can forget to breathe but I can't forget even a moment spent with you.

Mahirah: Awwwww!!! I was missing all this so much. Thank you for making my birthday special! You know you're just like my secret super hero.

Saad: That's really sweet. May I know how?

Mahirah: Cuz you disappear right when I need you. Hahaha….

Saad: Well…. Does that mean you need me?

Mahirah: (*after a minute of awkward silence*) No, I mean…. Well you were busy with **"Some stuffs"** right? And came here just to wish me and you did so get lost now.

Saad: (*In a teasing manner *) Ohh yes!!! I had few things actually to complete. I think it's time for me to leave and you should also enjoy your day. So byeee! Have a good day.

Mahirah: Wait…. How can I have a good day without you?

Saad: ummmm… Are you flirting?

Mahirah: Nahh, I am not flirting. I'm just trying to be extra nice for the person who is extra charming.

Saad: I get you, I get you….

(*Both laugh*)

Mahirah celebrated her birthday happily. She was so glad after talking to him. After a while, she posted her birthday pictures with her friends. When Saad saw the post, he felt so jealous about the people around her.

Saad: How was your birthday?

Mahirah: It went pretty well. I enjoyed the day so much

Saad: Ya! Definitely. Why wouldn't you enjoy? There were many people around you wishing you a happy birthday, laughing with you, hugging you, etc....

Mahirah: Well they're my friends but I don't feel the connection as how I feel with you. But it seems like you're jealous of them. Aren't you?

Saad: No... I mean.... Well, to be honest I am jealous of every single person who get to see you every day, whom you smile at and each and every laugh of yours which I don't hear.

Mahirah: Honestly, it feels good hearing this! I don't know why.

After this conversation, Mahirah's feelings for Saad became even more stronger but she was still not sure that it's just as a friend or more than that. No matter what, she was still loving his company and she just wanted to enjoy the phase of this strange but beautiful connection they have.

"Some bonds are meant to be, doesn't matter how, when, where but it's just meant to be.... You might never imagine someone out of your locality but everything what's meant for you will find a way to reach you."

Chapter – 2

The Conflict

**"There's no relationship without a conflict,
and There's no conflict without love."**

Few months passed, and everything was going pretty well. Saad decided to open up about his friendship with Mahirah to one of his close friends named Haris. He told him everything about her and confessed that he gave genuine feelings for her.

Saad: I genuinely feel that she's the one for me. I've never been this comfortable with someone ever before. The way she talks, the way she is, everything is just so beautiful about her. She's the one with whom I wanna spend my life with.

Haris: That's really good that you love her so much. But does she feel the same?

Saad: Not yet, but I will make her fall in love with me. I'll be the guy she wants in her life. I'll do everything for her. I won't give her any reason to complaint. Even after that if she doesn't feel the same then it's up to her, I don't have any right to force her.

Haris: I totally understand what you feel for her but I would suggest you should re-think about this.

Saad: But why? I've been thinking about her the whole day and after a lot of thoughts I've come to this conclusion.

Haris: Yes, I agree and totally get you. But I feel that she's totally opposite of you. You're a religious person, you don't like to socialize much with people and she's a content creator which means she'll have to interact with the opposite gender too, she's just totally opposite of you which might create Conflicts between both of you later. So please re- think about it.

Saad: Ya… don't worry about that. I'll re-think about it and let you know.

Even though Haris suggested him out of concern but those thoughts were stuck to his mind. He didn't know what to do. After a while, he thought of discussing this with Mahirah cuz he felt only it can now either solve this or end this. Instead of hanging by a thread, discussing with her might be better solution. So he texted her and started the conversation by asking her few religious questions. Mahirah felt strange and asked him about the reason behind him asking such questions so he replied:

Saad: Actually I am a religious person and almost everyone around me is religious too. So I just wanted to suggest you as a friend at least to not post yourself on social media as it's against our religion and not safe either as anyone can misuse your pictures.

Reading these texts made Mahirah mad at him. She became so pissed off and without thinking anything she replied:

Mahirah: Even my parents never interfere in my personal life. So who are you to say this to me? It's my choice to be a content creator and I won't stop this no matter what happens. You better mind your own business.

Saad became extremely disheartened and dejected by her words. He started feeling that Haris was right. It was his fault to have feelings and to care about her. So he apologized for interfering in her life and they ended the chat.

They didn't talk for almost a week. Neither did he text her nor she. After few days one of Mahirah's fellow creator friend Afra fell prey to the social media trap as someone hacked her page and misused her pictures even though when she barely had any post which reveals her face or identity. After this incident, Mahirah realized that he was not totally wrong. It's an Era of AI where such things are very common.

She should have at least given him a chance to prove his point instead of yelling at him.

But will she apologize for her mistake? Will they ever talk again or their story will come to an end? Let's read the next chapter to know what happens next.

"Sometimes even medicines can't heal a person as well as pure love can. It doesn't always require to be a lover to heal someone. If you love someone deep inside, even a single drop of tears while addressing them in prayer will act a strong barrier between them and all the problems they have. At the same time, it also has the capability to hurt a person so bad that it's wound may bleed for years."

Chapter – 3

The Realization

"Not every couple require to be the
same as each other, sometimes even the
contradictory pair creates a match like the
moon and stars."

Both Mahirah and Saad were guilt ridden. They wanted to apologize to each other but didn't had the courage to do so. As a result, both of them decided to give it a shot and implement what they said. So from the next day Mahirah started to pray her daily prayers without missing any and started to practice her religion and know more about it. On the other hand, Saad also tried to implement things in his life too. He tried socializing with people and being an outgoing person. Both of kind were satisfied with the result. Mahirah started to love being a religious person, she felt that connection with God and at each and every prayer she makes dua about him too and her eyes gets filled with tears. She didn't know exactly about the feeling but she felt a strong connection between him and her. She was thankful to him for making her religious cuz only a true one will try to make both of your lives best, here and hereafter. And Saad also enjoyed being a social person as it boosted his confidence and made him even a better person than he was before. But even after socializing with people and making friends he was still stuck thinking about Mahirah the whole time.

Few days passed, Mahirah thought of discussing these things with Afra as she was the one who asked her about Long Distance relationship once. Mahirah told Afra about everything that happened since day one and replied:

Afra: Do you feel something for him which you've never experienced before?

Mahirah: Yes, I've a weirdly strong feeling for him which I never had for anyone else before. Even though we don't talk nowadays but I can't stop thinking about him, addressing him in my prayers. He's runs in my mind 24/7.

Afra: Honestly, I feel that he's a good person at heart and he genuinely cares for you. That's the reason why he suggested you to become religious but without even thinking once, you started yelling at him. And the things which you told him might have hurt him so much. Nowadays most of the people around us support us even if we're wrong, no one thinks about the hereafter and if someone does, it means that he's a true one. Without thinking of himself or what you'll feel about him, he prioritized you, thought of your betterment. No one does it nowadays.

Mahirah: I regret everything I did. And I truly feel that he was right. I want to apologize to him but I don't know he might accept the apology or not.

Afra: I think you should go ahead and talk to him. What if he's not texting you for the same reason? Never think of the result if you didn't even take the initial step.

Mahirah: Yes, I'll definitely apologize for my mistakes. But……. it's actually not just about apologizing….

Afra: I knew it. You want to confess him about your feelings, right?

Mahirah: Yes **(*in a timid tone*)** But I don't know that he feels the same or not. And also, we're totally opposite of each other so he might not accept my feelings.

Afra: First of all……… JUST STOP OVERTHINKING JUST GO AND DISCUSS THESE THINGS WITH HIM. Don't confess directly but ask him in an indirect manner. Overthinking and wasting your time here won't solve your problem.

Mahirah: Sorry babe…. and thank you so much for making me feel much better and helping me out. Lovee youuu!!!

Afra: Love you too but I guess according to the situation, it's better for you to say it to him instead of me. **(*in a teasing manner*)**

Mahirah: Stop it… I am blushing….

Mahirah felt so much better talking to Afra. But she was so nervous texting him and was just wondering what he'll think about her, whether he'll reply or not etc but she recollected Afra's words and then dropped him a text asking for apology. Few minutes later he replied:

Saad: Why are you feeling sorry? I apologise for my mistake. I just blabbered anything without even thinking. I am really sorry for it.

Mahirah: No, actually you were right. I was the one who over reacted. I am sorry for it. Let's end this topic here. Ummmm…… Can I ask you something?

Saad: Sure. Please go ahead.

Mahirah: Can we be friends again?

Saad: I am glad that you asked this. I don't have any grudges against you. You were and will always be my friend. But it might be difficult for you to continue cuz we both are so different.

Mahirah: This world consists 8 billion people and each and everyone is different. So are we. I wouldn't have continued if I would be the same as before but your absence thought me a lot of things and changed me a lot as a person and I feel it's not necessary to be exactly same as each other. Sometimes being different adds an extraordinary flavour to the relationship. It separates us from the rest. I would love to continue our friendship.

Saad: I am extremely overwhelmed by your thoughts. Each and every single word of yours means a lot to me. Thank you so much. I am so glad to have you back.

They continue to chat for an hour and then winded up for the day. They both had feelings for each other they had no idea that both of them feel the same. They even started praying Tahajjud (mid-night prayer) and ask God for his/her love. Little did they know that the destiny has already planned everything for them. They're just playing their roles in their story. Mahirah shared everything with Afra and was very thankful for her as if she would not motivate her then they both might never be able to talk ever again. Now all that she wanted was him as her future. Let's see whether her dream will come true or not.

"Destiny is just like a director of
a movie and you're the central
character. You never know who the
director will choose as your leading
partner. Your part is just to play
your roles efficiently."

Chapter – 4

Beginning of a New Bond

"I am not aware of my future but I am definitely sure that it will begin and end with you."

Their bond turns even more strong each and every day. They both were enjoying this phase of their relationship. It was just like a new beginning to their bond where they fight, flirt, roast and annoy each other. Unlike other relationships where fight causes distance between two people, they get even more closer after every fight. Their daily conversation looks just like two best friends falling in love each other but who cares about the love, they'll still make fun of each other. The way they care for each other was too different but cute at the same time, such people raise our standards high in love. Once Mahirah was feeling emotional after watching a movie at so she texted him to share her feelings:

Mahirah: You alive?

(*waits for 2 minutes*)

Mahirah: You better text me within 5 minutes or else I'll kill you.

(*4.55 seconds later*)

Saad: The person you're texting is currently dead. Please try again later. Thank you.

Mahirah: Stop talking rubbish. I came here to bewail my woes and troubles. Lemme do that first

Saad: But we just talked an hour back and you were alright. What happened out of a sudden?

Mahirah: You won't even believe what happened. I was watching a movie and it's so emotional I can't even tell you. I feel so sad for the character in the movie. What if the same happens to me in future?

Saad: Yes, you're right.

Mahirah: You mean it will happen with me too in future? Do you even know how painful it was for her in the movie?

Saad: No, I meant you were right. I actually can't believe that you're crying over a movie. By the way you know, one of my friends is gonna get married and it's a destination wedding in Switzerland.

Mahirah: Woww!! That sounds great. Switzerland is one of my dream destinations you know. Are you gonna attend their wedding? I don't think so that you would cuz ferrets are not allowed in flights mostly.

Saad: Did you just call me a ferret?

Mahirah: Yes, I did. Asking this again won't make any difference in my words ferret.

Saad: If I am ferret then you're a Jill.

Mahirah: I am already emotional and upset watching the movie and you're here calling me a Jill. You don't understand me anymore. Get lost. I don't want to talk to you

Saad: But you started it first. I don't know why I am sorry for, but I would like to apologize mam. Sorry, it's all my mistake.

Mahirah: Ya, much better now. It's okay just don't repeat it again ferret.

Saad: You called me ferret again……

Mahirah: Can't you see that I am upset for the movie.

Saad: No, I can't cuz you don't look like upset from any angle.

Mahirah: It's all because of you. I came here to share my emotions but you distracted and destroyed my emotional mood. Now how will I get that glow on my face which I usually get after crying?

Saad: You don't need any glow cuz you already shine brighter than the moon in the sky.

Mahirah: Cuz you're the beautiful night I shine for.

Saad: How sweet…. it's all my influence on you so all the credit goes to me. Thank you. 😊

Mahirah: You're not a deserving candidate to flirt with.

Saad: Ohh really? Pardon mam. Can you then please let me know who's the right one then? 😊

Mahirah: Anyone in this whole world except you.

Saad: (*jealous*) Go and talk to someone else then.

Mahirah: Nahh…. you're enough.

They have such playful arguments everyday. Even they don't understand that how and when they change each other's mood. It's such a strange but beautiful bond. Whenever any one is upset, the other one is always there to cheer him up. They both never felt such connection with anyone else ever before. They were so thankful to have each other in their lives. Their bond didn't just bring them closer, but also closer to God.

After few days, Saad received an offer letter from a multinational company with high package than the current one but it was a full-time job so he wouldn't be able to spend much time with Mahirah. He was not able to come to a conclusion whether to accept the offer or not. So he thought of discussing it with her. He told her everything about the offer:

Mahirah: I feel that you should accept the offer as comparatively it has a better package than the current one.

Saad: Ya, even I am thinking to accept it but the only issue is that I won't be able to spend much time with you and I've experienced many friends turning to a stranger cuz of lack of communication and I don't want to experience the same with you.

Mahirah: That's really so sweet that you think a lot about us but at this point I think you should prioritize your career first. And you really think that our bond is so weak that it can break by this reason? DEFINITELY NOTT! We're just like two river streams that are meant to meet at the end. So don't worry at all about it and don't anymore time. Just accept the offer.

Saad: Thanks a Ton for helping me out to make a better decision. You're a saviour. I will try my best to spend as much time with you as I can.

Mahirah was quite happy for him but also a little upset at the same time. So she thought of completing all her work before he returns so that they can have a playful conversation just like before. They both end up completely exhausted but still make sure to spend some time with each other. They eventually started missing each other even more. They wanted to meet each other now, they were tired of being just virtually connected. But instead of just complaining, they were repeatedly asking God for a meet up and addressing each other in prayers. Will their prayers be answered? Let's continue reading to get this question answered first.

"Love is just like a magnet. No matter how far you are, it will find its way to connect if the bond is strong."

Chapter – 5

Love beyond Hardships

They both were not able to spend much time with each other but they had a good mutual understanding so even if they talked for an hour, they make sure that nothing goes wrong. Few days later, Mahirah got selected for a sponsored creator event which was in Delhi for 3 days. She realized that it's nothing but the answer to her prayers. She was so thankful to God and thought to book a ticket to Pune too and give him a surprise. But the air tickets were too expensive so she decided to book the flight from Delhi later when the event gets over. She did not tell him anything about the event so he had no clue that she's gonna travel to India as neither did she tell him nor she posted it anywhere. Mahirah was excited for the event but she was even more excited to meet him. But it was a creator event, so it was obvious for her to meet and collab with different creators. She packed everything and while packing she realized that she didn't bring any gift for him and she did not even know what to bring and she also couldn't ask his preference as it was a surprise. So she decided to select anything from the gift shop. She went to many gift shops but didn't like anything. She didn't want to go to men's shop as she would feel awkward but didn't have any other option left, so she had to. She entered a haberdashery shop, but she was feeling embarrassed asking a gift for a friend so she asked the salesman to show a presentable gift for her brother. This was her first time purchasing something from male's section but not the first time for the salesman so he understood that she wanted to gift someone special. So he asked her whether she would like to purchase any clothing item. She agreed so before showing her variant options he asked her few questions:

Salesman: Mam can I know the size of the clothes you would like to purchase for your brother?

Mahirah: (*awkwardness on its peak*) Actually I don't know the exact size but his age is 23 and I guess medium to large will be fine.

Salesman: Mam do you have any picture of your brother so can I have a clear idea about it.

Mahirah showed a picture of him and then he showed her a variety of options but she was so confused as all those clothes were looking great. But she was hesitant about the size and was not sure that he would like or not. As she has never seen him in person so she doesn't have any idea about the size of clothes he wears. So she dropped the idea of purchasing clothes for him. Then the salesman suggested her to check their few watch collections, she might like it. Mahirah agreed. But she didn't like those watches so he asked her:

Salesman: Mam we have a better collection in couple watches. Would you like to check that out?

Mahirah: (*blushes*) ya, that's also fine.

She finally selected a couple watch and gift wrapped it. She packed it and kept it in her hand luggage. The next day she left to the airport and was just thinking about him. She couldn't wait to meet him. She reached Delhi after a couple of hours and then checked in in the hotel. The event will start at evening so she got freshen up, had her lunch and took rest.

She woke up at 4 pm, got ready and reached there after an hour. She met many creators and friends in the event and was enjoying her time. In the same event there was a guy named Zayn who was staring at her since she entered. Mahirah had no clue about it. She was talking to her friends and enjoying the event.

After a while when she was sitting alone, Zayn approached her and said:

Zayn: Hey! I was noticing you for quite a while now. I just wanted to ask something if you don't mind.

Mahirah: Sure. Please go ahead.

Zayn: As you know it's a creator event so I wanted to ask for a collaboration with you. If you agree then we can go ahead with it tomorrow as the event will continue for 3 days.

Mahirah: Sure. No worries.

After few hours Mahirah was about to leave the event so she booked a cab. Zayn was just trying to impress her so he came and asked:

Zayn: Are you leaving?

Mahirah: Yes. Just waiting for my cab.

Zayn: Cab won't be safe at this time. If you want I can drop you.

Mahirah: No, it's okay. I'll manage. Thank you.

Zayn: Don't worry. I'll drop you safely. You can cancel the cab if you want.

Mahirah was not completely ready to go with him but it was getting late and the cab was taking time too so she agreed. Mahirah sat in the back seat to which Zayn said:

Zayn: Front seat is much more comfortable than the back seat, if you want you can have a seat.

Mahirah: No, I am really comfortable Here. Thank you.

Zayn: It's up to you.

Zayn tried talking to her while driving but Mahirah was not much interested so he dropped her and left. Mahirah was too tired after coming from the event so she just slept.

The next day when she woke up and checked her phone, she saw Saad's texts.

Saad: Where were you yesterday? I missed you so much. Didn't call you cuz I thought you might be busy.

Mahirah: I missed you too. Actually I was kind of busy with all the work and after completing everything I was so tired that I slept so I couldn't text you.

Saad: That's fine. But at least inform me before you get disappeared for a whole day cuz I get worried. Then I am not able to do anything except thinking about you the whole day. Cuz it's important to keep updates about your pets.

Mahirah: How funny! (*sarcastically*)

Saad: You find my feelings funny? Couldn't you reply to the rest of the text and replied only for this. How rude! (*emotional drama*)

Mahirah: Sorry……. But wait. Doing all this drama is my job not yours. So you better stop it.

Saad: Yes, I know. I was just letting you taste your own medicine. How was it? **(*in a teasing manner*)**

Mahirah: Not good at all 😭.

They continued their conversation, after a few minutes Mahirah recollected that she forgot to ask him his address and she can't ask directly so she'll have to make an excuse or ask him indirectly

Mahirah: By the way, I've never asked for your address. Let's exchange addresses.

Saad felt weird but agreed to it and they both exchanged their addresses. They both winded up for the day. Mahirah got freshen up and was thinking to book a flight day after tomorrow. At the same time someone rang the bell. She opened the door and it was Zayn. Mahirah didn't how Zayn came suddenly without informing her. But she didn't say him anything cuz she didn't want to hurt anyone and asked him to come inside. She went to the reception to order breakfast for him but mistakenly left her phone in the room. While she was in the reception, she got a call from Saad and Zayn picked it up and asked who's on the call to which Saad replied:

Saad: I am Mahirah's friend. May I know who's this? And Where's she?

Zayn understood that he might be someone close to Mahirah as she has saved his number as 'Fav Notification' so he replied:

Zayn: I am Mahirah's best friend. But who are you? She never spoke about you to me.

Saad was hurted hearing this, he wondered why didn't she ever spoke anything about him or any male friend she has but without asking anything he just replied with

Saad: Please ask her to call me back when she returns. Thank you.

After this he hung up the call. When Mahirah came back she saw her phone in Zayn's hand and asked him what was he doing with her phone. Zayn started making excuses and replied:

Zayn: Nothing I was just looking at the phone case it's beautiful.

Mahirah felt strange and suspicious about him so she checked the phone and found out that Saad called her and it was a received call. So she understood that he picked up the call so she yelled at Zayn for doing so. Zayn apologized but he wanted to know about the relationship between him and her so he asked:

Zayn: I apologize for my mistake but can I know who he was? Is he someone really close to you?

Mahirah was already pissed off at him and when she heard this she got even more angry so she said:

Mahirah: It's none of your business. You better mind your own and you better leave now cuz I don't want to utter anything which will make me feel guilty. So it's better for you to leave.

Zayn left her place and Mahirah was stressed thinking about Saad as she thought he might have misunderstood her. She didn't have the guts to call him as she felt that it was her fault. So she decided to apologize to him by meeting him personally. So she booked the flight to Pune which was the next day. Will Saad accept the apology? What will happen next? Let's solve this mystery.

"Trust & Understanding are the two main pillars of a relationship. If any of the two gets weaken, you'll never be able to last it longer."

Chapter – 6

Just a Flight Away

"The moon might be surrounded with billions of stars, but it is still doesn't shine brighter than mine."

The very next day Mahirah left to the airport. She did not think anything about the event, herself or any other person. She was just concerned about Saad. She didn't want to lose him at any cost. It was a rushed hour so everything was gridlocked. She got panicked that she'll be able to reach the airport on time or not. She was totally stuck in the traffic.

Couple of hours later, she reached the airport somehow and heard the last call of her flight. She completed all the process as fast as she could and finally got into the plane. She was the last passenger as she reached just 3 minutes before the time of departure. She felt much better now cuz she didn't miss her flight but she was still stressed thinking about him. After few minutes when the plane took off from the runway, she was amused with the beautiful view from the plane. She then moved back and was completely lost into his thoughts, thinking about how he would look in real, what will be his reaction, recollecting all the conversations they had, all these thoughts were making her smile and blush. She couldn't just wait anymore to meet him. After a while, when the air hostess was serving the beverages, she asked Mahirah her preference. And Mahirah was so lost into his thoughts that she was not even answering. The air hostess tried calling her again:

Air hostess: Mam can you please let me know what would you like to have?

Mahirah got distracted from her thoughts and answered:

Mahirah: Ohh, I am really very sorry! I would like to have a tea. How much should I pay for it?

Air hostess: No mam, it's a complimentary service by us.

Mahirah: The amount I've paid for the ticket, you're supposed to provide a list of complimentary services.

Mahirah replied……… in her thoughts. What she actually said was:

Mahirah: Thank you

2 hours later she reached Pune Airport. She was feeling so excited and nervous at the same time. She got her luggage and went to the washroom to freshen up. When she came back she found that one of her luggage is missing. She got stressed. She checked it everywhere and asked the security about it but they were unable to find. The security asked him to file a complaint at missing centre but it will consume lot of time so she'll have to wait there. She then thought for a while and decided not to file any complaint as she didn't want to waste her time in these things. She just wanted to meet him and clear all the misunderstandings. If she would have lost the luggage in which she had gift for him then she would definitely wait for eternity but the gift was secured with her so she decided not to wait and leave to his place. She booked a cab and gave him the address. It was a long journey. She was so tired travelling from so long. She didn't know that Pune is such a huge city with Never-ending and numerous mountains. There were no food stalls or any shop nearby. So she asked the driver about it and asked him to stop not any food court first as she was feeling empty. So after a journey of 2 hours she reached at the food court. It was so crowded and strange for her as everyone were speaking in Marathi. She went to one of the stalls and the salesman asked her in Marathi first:

Sales man: Tumhala kaye order karayace aahe?

She hardly understood anything except for the word order and she assumed that he's asking what would you like to order which is right so she somehow managed to order breakfast. While she was having her breakfast, she noticed someone talking in Hindi with the same salesman. She said to herself "It just slipped from my mind that this is India so it's obvious for people to speak Hindi, I simply made myself embarrassed".

After having breakfast, she resumed her journey to meet him. After 3 hours she reached his location. Her heart was beating out of control, she was trying to calm down but she couldn't believe that she's finally going to meet him. She's just in front of his home. She went inside the building and rang the bell. Waited for a few minutes and then he opened the door.

Both were just in front of each other and couldn't believe their eyes. They were just speechless. They were just standing and staring each other at the door for more than 15 minutes now. Then, Mahirah asked:

Mahirah: Won't you ask me to come in?

Saad was just lost into her eyes so he couldn't hear what she said so she asked him again:

Mahirah: May I come in?

Saad was so mesmerized by her beauty, her voice, just everything about her that he still didn't hear a single word. Mahirah was actually liking this behavior but she didn't want him to know about it. So she said in a loud tone this time:

Mahirah: Either you let me come in or I'll leave. You better respond this time or else it won't be good for you 😤.

Saad: Ohh! sorry! I am really very sorry! Please come in. Have a seat.

Mahirah: Much better. THANK YOU!

He was totally speechless he didn't utter a single word. After a while, Mahirah asked:

Mahirah: Did you recognize me?

Saad: How can I not? I have never known or seen such a beautiful person in my whole life. But how did you reach here? You didn't even inform me. I guess that's the reason why you were not replying to my texts.

Mahirah: That's really so sweet of you. Actually I wanted to give you a surprise that's why I didn't tell you anything about it neither did I reply you cuz I am not good in hiding things so I would have just ended up saying you everything about it.

Saad: You literally just made my day. I feel so blessed to see you, to have you, to be able to spend time with you.

Mahirah felt so good hearing this. She realized that she was just overthinking, he did not misunderstand her. If there was something such, she would have understood by his behaviour. They had a conversation for almost half an hour, she told him all about the event, why she had to come to India and then she decided to give him a surprise and after than She asked him about it to clear everything.

Mahirah: Saad actually I wanted to ask you something regarding the person who picked the phone. I know you might have misunderstood me but trust me I met him just in the event and he's not even My friend. I mistakenly left My phone there and he picked. Do you still hold any grudges against me? I am really very sorry for everything. I didn't mean to hurt you.

Saad: I don't need any justification cuz I know that you are not wrong. Yes, I was hurt at that time but I just had a gut feeling that you'll never do something which will hurt me so I felt much better and you travelled this long to meet me so how can I hold any grudges against you. In fact I feel so blessed. This is the best day ever.

Mahirah was so overwhelmed hearing this. Her love and respect for him increased. She wanted to confess her feelings. But before she could do that, she received a text from Zayn apologizing and asking her for a date. Mahirah's mood suddenly changed and she became upset. Saad noticed the sudden change in her so asked her about the reason. Mahirah showed the text to him. Saad just smiled and said,

Saad: Leave all these. Just tell me why are you worried? Do you really think that our bond is so weak that these things can affect it? No Mahirah. You're special! We're special! I don't care even if hundreds of people or the whole world tries to put you down or prove you wrong. I'll still not believe it until you say it by your own. If you were wrong, you wouldn't have travelled this long to meet me, you wouldn't say everything to me, you would never listen to me but you did, you did everything for us. And these all things mean so much to me. I don't know what I am to you, but for me. You're everything.

Mahirah felt so emotional and blessed hearing this cuz she had many friends by her side but never had such a person who's with her at any cost just like a shadow. She hugged him and said:

Mahirah: I love you! I love you so much. You mean so much to me. I wanted to confess all these since so long but I didn't know how you will react. But I feel this is the right time. You mean so much to me not just as a friend but more than that. I want you till the end. I love you a lot.

Saad hugged her back and confessed his feelings too. He replied:

Saad: I had a crush on you since the beginning. The reason why I stopped texting you before your birthday was my feelings for you which increases each and everyday. I love you so much. And I'll always do.

Both of them finally confessed their feelings. They were so Glad to know that they both felt for each other but didn't had the guts to confess it, thinking it will spoil their bond. After few minutes, Mahirah asked him:

Mahirah: But I am so worried thinking about our future. Will we be able to marry each other? Will our parents approve this marriage?

Saad: Instead of worrying about future, why not work hard to make it happen? Rest he'll manage who makes the impossible, possible. Did we ever think that we'll fall in love with someone totally opposite to us in every possible way, not just the city but the whole country differs and we will even meet? It's all written. And it's possible for us to meet, then it's also possible for us to marry each other. What we just need is to work hard and to prove that we both deserve each other.

Mahirah: You amaze me every time. I've never felt so lucky in my entire life. I love you!

Saad: If I want you as my partner so I've to improve so that I can be a well deserving partner for you.

Both of them had conversation for hours. They have never experienced such a beautiful feeling ever. Mahirah realized that she forgot to give him the gift she bought for him. Saad loved the watch so much but as it was a couple watch so he asked:

Saad: As it's a couple watch so should I understood that you manifested us together?

Mahirah: I guess it's just how Manifesting to God works.

Both Mahirah and Saad had a beautiful time together. They thought to celebrate their first meeting by going for an outing. But they would come back late, and Mahirah didn't know where to stay for few days and they can't live together so they booked a room near his home.

They went for shopping, purchased gifts for each other, clicked pictures together, etc. They spent almost 3 hours in the mall and it was too late so they thought to have dinner and then go back home. Saad took her to a restaurant, pulled the chair out for her and asked her to have a seat. He ordered food for both of them. While the food was getting ready, they were expressing their feelings towards each other. He went on his knees and proposed to her. He said:

Saad: I am so thankful to God who blessed me by sending you in my life. I am thankful for each and every day you've been with me. I am thankful for each and everything you did for me. Thank you so much. I will always love you, no matter what. Will you accept my love for you and love me the same way back??

Mahirah was just about to reply but at the same, Saad's brother saw him proposing her.

ng someone is easy, but

ur love, committing to

on for the entire life

the

ed to someone just

, that's where

....

fail."

"You entered my life just like a
beautiful Dream and fulfilling
dreams is my last Destination
with you......."

"Loving someone is easy, but proving your love, committing to that one person for the entire life and being devoted to someone just like a newlywed, that's where most people fail."

To Be continued……

"You entered my life just like a beautiful Dream and fulfilling the dreams is my last Destination… with you……"

Please note that this is my first book so there might be mistakes. The Story will be continued in the next part of the book. Please share your reviews by scanning this QR code below. It will be appreciated.

Thank you